When Love Lies Bleeding

by

Candy Denman

A Novella inspired by the film 'The Third Man'

Published by City Fiction

This is a work of fiction. Names, characters, businesses, places, events and incidents are either the products of the author's imagination or used in a fictitious manner. Any resemblance to actual persons, living or dead, or actual events is purely coincidental.

ISBN: 978-1-910040-34-8

WHEN LOVE LIES BLEEDING

For most people San Francisco meant flowers in your hair, hippies and Steve McQueen driving a Mustang GT over the road humps; or, for those too young or too stoned to remember the sixties: Golden Gate, Alcatraz and cable cars. But for me it meant Cassie. She was the only thing of importance to me there, or anywhere, and when the opportunity came up to cover a story in the city, I jumped at the chance. And what a story it turned out to be.

The world-wide flu pandemic of the moment was killing people everywhere, but nowhere in the first world had been hit as hard as the West Coast of America. It wasn't so much the number of people infected; it was the rate at which they were dying that had surprised everyone. The world, and, more importantly, news hungry Americans, particularly those living on the West Coast, or with loved ones living there, wanted to know why. As the nominal science correspondent for my East Coast based paper, and the only reporter there to have lived in San Francisco, I was the obvious choice to send and cover the story. At least, that's what I told myself. There was also the little problem of my 'personality clash' with the editor, as we euphemistically called his giving me every shit job that came up since he found out I'd screwed his old lady. The fact that almost everyone had screwed his wife at one time or another didn't seem to make the situation any better. Perhaps she'd told him I was a better lover than he was or some such. Anyway he was sending me to San Francisco, possibly to get me away from her, or maybe because he was secretly hoping I'd get the flu and die. Maybe I was mad to say yes, no one sane was travelling to the West Coast, in fact, people were leaving in droves, but the thought of getting away from the atmosphere in the office, not to mention the chance to get some sunshine and maybe see my ex-girlfriend Cassie, was too good to be missed.

I tried to get hold of a course of the anti-viral tablets recommended for this new strain of flu before leaving. The tablets were called *Zeroflu* and there had been jokes on social media about it being zero pills as it was in real short supply and only being given out to those who were diagnosed with the disease and who had other medical conditions making them at risk. It wasn't readily available to those who were generally fit and voluntarily putting themselves in danger of catching it. The nurse who gave me my flu vaccination before I left warned me that it would take two weeks to work and wouldn't cover me against the current strain anyway. It seems the vaccine makers, like the antiviral treatment makers had been caught on the hop by this one, as they had been by the bird and swine flu pandemics in earlier years. Janice, the paper's organizer, gave me my tickets along with a bottle of sanitizing hand gel and a leaflet on how to avoid catching flu. The leaflet seemed to suggest my only hope was to stay home and not go anywhere people might be and definitely nowhere near a doctor or a hospital. She reminded me to phone in my reports daily and wished me luck. She seemed sincere.

I read up about the pandemic as we flew across the country, the numbers with the infection, the numbers dying, but my mind kept going back to Cassie and what it would be like to see her again after all this time.

We were both students when we met, even in a campus full of beautiful people she seemed more alive than anyone else, more vibrant, and she made me feel that way too. We were way too young for a lasting relationship. At least, that's what everyone told me, my parents included, but I didn't care. I wanted us to get married straight away. She turned me down flat. I might have been ready to settle into family life, but she wasn't. She was excited by the world and all the possibilities ahead. She wanted to experience everything - and everyone. I should have walked away then, but I was prepared to be kept on a string, handy to have around when she needed a presentable date, to spend time with when no one better was available or someone to help her when she was in trouble. I was in love.

True to form, Cassie didn't answer her phone when I rang to tell her I was coming to San Francisco. I left a message and sent her an email giving her my flight details, asking her if she could meet me at the airport or maybe come to where I was staying. I even sent her a text with all the details; I know, I know, I wasn't exactly playing hard to get. Unsurprisingly, I didn't get a response to any of it. Nothing new there, either. It wasn't like we regularly kept in touch, just the odd card on anniversaries and birthdays, from me, usually unacknowledged, but I'd kept track of where she was, what she was doing. I guess you could say I was a bit of a stalker. When I checked before leaving, it turned out she was working for a large pharmaceutical company. The same company that made *Zeroflu*, the only effective antiviral treatment for this current outbreak of flu. The treatment that I had failed to get my hands on. Of course, it occurred to me that she could be a good source of information, not to mention *Zeroflu*, but I didn't tell her that on the phone, even on the third message I left her. I spun her a line about wanting to catch up with her, about wanting to see her again. As a friend. I didn't know if she had a partner, a lover or whatever who might listen to her messages and I didn't want to screw that up, not before I arrived, anyway. I asked her to email me her address although not getting a reply didn't really matter, I knew where she lived. I'm a journalist; I knew how to find these things out.

We landed just after eleven and taxied to the stand. I looked out of the small window, eager for a sight of the sun after the cold, grey East Coast weather I had left behind, but the sky was heavy with cloud and it was threatening to rain. Before we were allowed to disembark, a public health employee wearing a heavy-duty mask and overalls came in and sprayed the half-empty cabin to kill any viruses we might be bringing with us, ironic when you think that San Francisco was the infectious area, not Springfield, Massachusetts from where we had set out that morning. As I walked across the airport concourse, I was to get my first real taste of the fear gripping the city; everyone was wearing paper masks, even though a report had shown them to be next to useless in stopping the infection spreading.

I don't know why I had ever hoped she might be, but Cassie wasn't waiting at the arrivals area when I finally got my luggage and got through to the main concourse. I checked out the waiting areas and cafes, but there was no sign of her anywhere.

'Joe!' I heard and turned around, disappointed that the voice calling my name had been definitely masculine and therefore, definitely not Cassie. A man hurried over, pulling down his paper mask and I recognised Martin, a journalist I had worked with many years ago, when we were both young and hungry. It seemed a very long time ago.

'Good to see you.' I said, trying to hide my disappointment and held out my hand.

Martin held up his hands and stepped back.

'Whoa! I don't shake hands anymore. That's one of the ways this bug spreads.' He explained. 'Physical contact is a no-no. You here to cover the story?'

The story, no need to say which one, as he pulled his mask back up.

'Yeah, you?'

'Yeah, just arrived from New York, I'm with the Times now, did you know?' His voice was slightly muffled but there was no disguising his pride in saying where he worked. To me. Of course, I knew he was with the Times. He knew it too. We both went for the same job and he got it. I went to Springfield not NY.

'Sure.' I said, and resisted the urge to punch him on the nose.

'Say, I'm at the Four Seasons, where're you at?'

'I need to check my emails; I'm not sure where they've booked me yet.' I lied rather than admit I was staying somewhere considerably cheaper. I saw a glint of pleasure in Martin's eye and the crease of his mask suggested the smirk underneath. He understood my situation perfectly and clearly took pleasure from being higher up the food chain. He was such a dick.

'We should meet up. Have a drink, you say where

as you know the area.' He was shamelessly going to milk me for local knowledge and contacts. He knew that. I knew that. And we both knew I wouldn't let it happen.

'Sure. I'll give you a call,' I said, but I'd already lost him, with a wave of his hand he was hurrying towards someone more important than an old friend, colleague and one-time rival.

Resigned to the fact that Cassie wasn't there to meet me, I tried calling her as I waited in the taxi queue. Needless to say, there was no reply and I left a message, telling her where I was staying and asking her to get back to me. I didn't hold out much hope, Cassie had never been good at getting back to me. It was one of her more endearing traits.

The hotel was surprisingly full, unlike the more exclusive ones which relied on tourism and were struggling. You couldn't blame people for wanting to keep their distance from the plague, as some more irresponsible tabloids were dubbing the outbreak. I consoled myself with the thought that The Times were only putting Martin in such an expensive hotel because they got a reduced rate. My own place was not out to impress anyone, it was an identikit mid-range business hotel that could have been in any city, but it was clean and it had a bar. There were a few other reporters staying there but in the main it was TV backroom crews and a whole bunch of serious grey-suited men. It seemed the only people in this part of the city were journalists and public health officials, all trying to find out what the hell was going on and they were easy to tell apart. The health group were trying hard to avoid the journalists, not because they didn't want to answer questions but because the newshounds were all drinking and trying to find ways around the strict California anti-smoking laws. It was a close call as to whether they were more frightened of breathing in second-hand smoke than catching the flu.

I dumped my bag in my room, and after I'd checked in with my paper and got the latest news on the situation from CNN, I went downtown to pick up a press info pack from the Department of Public Health building in Grove Street, I didn't want to miss a press briefing even if they were unlikely to tell me anything I didn't already know. Duty done, I checked my watch. It was four-thirty. Cassie would be finishing work for the day soon, and if I knew her half as well as I thought I did, she would be taking the ferry back to the city from her office in Oakland. She had never understood why people commuted to work in cars when they could do it on a boat. As someone who felt queasy just looking at the water, I understood it all too well. The ferry crossing could get pretty rough in the winter months. But it was a nice afternoon, well, the rain had stopped anyway, and if I hurried, I'd catch her as she got off the boat and could walk with her back to her home. At least, that was the plan, I didn't want to reveal that I already knew her latest address; I didn't want to scare her off. But, as I watched countless ferries arrive and scanned the commuters hurrying along the pier and out of the turnstiles, there was no Cassie. Like at the airport, many people were masked and I wondered if I had missed her, but I knew her walk, the way she moved, I couldn't believe I would not have recognised her even with her face covered.

I left another message on her phone with no expectation of a reply. I told myself that I had no choice; I would have to go to her home and field the awkward questions about how I knew where she lived and try not to make myself seem too desperate to see her. Even if that was the way I felt.

Her apartment was in a small block in a sought-after area near Lafayette Park, a short bus ride from the pier. She must have been doing well; there was no way I would have been able to afford it. I pushed the buzzer next to her apartment number, there was no name on it, but there weren't for half the buttons in the block. There was no reply. I rang again with the same result and then started pressing the buttons for every apartment in the block. I hadn't made it even halfway through before someone buzzed me in. So much for security. Cassie's apartment was on the second floor, and when I got there, I could hear someone talking inside. A man's voice, speaking Spanish in a harsh and angry tone. That made me pause, but not for long. The response was quieter, pleading, placating, I couldn't make out if it was a man or a woman, but it was enough to make my mind up. I was her old friend, and even if this angry man was her partner and I was about to make things worse, I couldn't just turn and go, not when she could be in trouble.

I banged on the door.

'Hey, Cassie! It's me, Joe. Are you okay?' I called out and was met by a tense silence and then some urgent whispering.

'It's me, your old friend Joe? I said I was coming?' I carried on, in a friendly tone that belied the feeling of fear that was creeping up my belly. There was some more whispering and the sound of feet shuffling towards the door. I made sure I was wearing my friendliest smile as the door slowly opened a little and a small Hispanic man peered round it. He didn't look happy to see me, but I was used to that.

'You got the wrong place.' He said quickly and started to close the door.

'What happened? Did she move out?' I asked him, still making nice while putting my foot in the door in the way they did in the movies and trying to see past him. His body was blocking the way and I could see nothing of the room behind.

'Yes. She move out. Last week.'

He went to close the door, but I leant in, pushing against it and trying to force it open. He had to move slightly to get his weight behind the door and in doing so; I got my first glimpse into the living room, and saw the other man in there. He was built like a tank and as he looked up, startled by my efforts to get in, I could see he was sifting through the contents of a box he held in one enormous, meaty hand.

'You go now!' The first man shouted, stamped on my foot and as I leapt back in pain, slammed the door shut. That hadn't gone quite the way it was supposed to and as I went back down the stairs, I tried to make sense of what little I had managed to get a look at. Back in college, Cassie and I had a friend who was a painter. He wasn't very good, but soon after he had presented Cassie with a picture, he had died in a car accident. The picture was apparently his interpretation of the bay, but you would never have known that from looking at it. His death gave the painting way more meaning that it would ever have had if he had lived and there was no way Cassie would have moved out and left her prized picture behind, but I was sure I had seen it on the wall. Nor would she have left the place in quite such a mess. Don't get me wrong, Cassie wasn't known for her tidiness, but most of her belongings seemed to have been scattered over the floor with empty drawers thrown haphazardly on top of their contents. No, it didn't take a master sleuth to realise that the men in Cassie's flat had been searching the place, and they didn't look like they were the police to me.

I limped to a less expensive part of town before going into a bar that looked like it was more my style than those around Cassie's neighbourhood, that is to say, it looked cheap and not very cheerful. The bar stools were worn down by the regular's butts and the counter was a little tacky when I leant on it but at least the barkeep didn't want to chat. He was probably pleased to have at least one customer, but if so, he didn't show it. I had decided to see if getting drunk would make the situation more understandable, but it didn't. So, I drank more and at some point, must have moved bars. I seemed to remember thinking that was a good idea.

I have no recollection of how I got back to the hotel, but I must have done so because I woke up there the next morning, fully clothed on my bed. I was no further forward with anything and I had a serious hangover to go with my confusion. Coffee, a hot shower and painkillers helped me to feel more human, but as I staggered into the days press briefing late and listened to the platitudes coming from the press officer advising people to wash their hands and stay home if they felt ill, I still hadn't come to a rational explanation as to why two Mexican's had been tossing Cassie's apartment, or for where she had gone, well, not an explanation that looked too healthy for her, anyway.

'Joe! I thought you wouldn't make it, given how drunk you were last night! I had to help you into a cab.' Martin supplied the explanation of how I had managed to get back to the hotel, I must have left my nice empty bar and gone to one frequented by colleagues, probably The Four Seasons if I had met up with Martin. Maybe I had needed someone to talk to, to feel less alone. Either way something told me, it hadn't been a good move.

'I don't know what shit you'd been taking but, man, you were coming out with some crazy stories.'

He slapped me on the back and I tried not to wince.

'Like what?' I said through gritted teeth.

'About your contact in the pharmaceutical company? That she'd gone missing and there were Mexicans involved somehow.'

I groaned. Inwardly, I hoped.

'Never could handle whiskey.' I said with a rueful smile and he laughed.

'No kidding. I mean, telling me she's been kidnapped by Mexicans? As if I'd believe that excuse!' He pointed a finger at me. 'So, when you find this contact, you'll let me know, right? And don't forget your promise to bring me along to your meeting with her.'

'You'll be the first to know.' I reassured him, lying through my teeth. I'd never let him meet a contact of mine, any contact, let alone Cassie, and I knew he was lying too when he said I had promised to do that. Even drunk there were things I knew I would never do, lines I would never cross, and that was one.

I dutifully filed my copy on the press conference and tried not to make it sound like there was nothing new to say, even if that was the truth. I had decided to take a trip over to Oakland and the pharmaceutical company where Cassie worked. She seemed to be hiding from me, or the Mexicans, and I felt I had no choice but to stop leaving phone messages for her to ignore and try and speak to her in person.

True to form, the weather had deteriorated and the ferry crossing didn't help my nausea. I stood on deck, pale and sweating, as other passengers wisely kept their distance, probably thinking that I was going down with the flu. Tell the truth, I felt so bad it crossed my mind that this was more than a hangover, then shook off that thought. Alcohol always makes me paranoid.

The pharmaceutical company building in Oakland was massive and modern, bright and shiny and clean, all glass and steel with fences around the site and guards sitting in booths by the gates leading into the car parks. On the website the building had looked shiny; gleaming in the sunshine, with beautifully manicured gardens, but today, in the rain, it just looked grey and dull, and the lawns had long since been replaced by tarmac, as if they had never been there at all. Being on foot, I was sure there would be ways I could get into the complex avoiding the guards, but I knew that I would encounter similar levels of security at the main building doors, so I approached the youngest looking guard, hoping he would be the most gullible and smiled in what I hoped was an unthreatening manner.

'Hi, I'm here to see Cassie Lowell. She works in the distribution centre.'

'And your name, sir?'

'Joe Hames.'

The guard checked his visitor sheet, thoroughly.

'You're not on the list, Sir.' He said politely.

'Really?' I feigned surprise and leaned over as if to check for myself. There were a lot of names, and, he was right, none were mine. No surprise there. I was relieved to see that Martin's name wasn't there either, so at least I hadn't told enough to get him here.

'She must have forgotten to let you know I was coming. Could you maybe give her a call? Tell her I'm here?'

The security guard frowned and turned to the second man who was busy checking cars through the barrier.

'Barry? This man -'

'Yeah, yeah,' Barry interrupted him and nodded to the driver of a gold Lexus and raised the barrier without even checking his ID, perhaps it was the CEO. 'Just call the front desk. They can deal with it.'

The young man made the call and was told to let me through to reception. I could feel him watching me all the way, making sure I didn't deviate from the route. Maybe I should have picked on the older guy who wasn't still keen on his work.

The lobby was all clean lines and minimalist furniture, a few chairs that looked more comfortable than they probably were and a coffee table covered in bright, shiny company brochures. I was told by the kid at the front desk to take a seat and someone would come down. There was no way I could sneak past her because, unsurprisingly, everyone had to use their ID card to open the half-height turnstiles in order to pass into the main body of the building. No card, no entry. So, I sat on the hard, bright, shiny chair and waited and as I waited, I tried to picture the Cassie I knew working in a place like this. It was hard. I wasn't exactly sure what she did in this place, her job title, Assurance and Operations Specialist, was suitably vague but it just didn't seem right for her, for the Cassie who was adorably unreliable and who craved excitement. I was willing to bet that there was very little excitement in assurance and operations.

As I sat there thinking, I became aware of a smartly dressed woman and a grey-suited man speaking quietly to each other and glancing over at me. Seeing that I had spotted them, they approached, the woman in the lead, and I stood up to meet them.

'I understand you are here to meet Miss Lowell?' the woman asked, straight to the point.

'Yes,' I said, 'I haven't had a message cancelling.' Which was true. I hadn't had a message confirming, either.

Something about their manner was awkward, embarrassed even.

'No,' the man started and looked for help from the woman.

'Are you a friend of hers, Mr -', she checked a post-it note in her hand, 'Mr Hames?'

'Yes, an old friend, as well as a business contact.' I didn't want to say what business. 'Is there a problem?' Something about the way they were behaving was screaming that there was.

The man cleared his throat, looked at the woman again and then, when he realised he wasn't going to get any help there, continued.

'I'm sorry to have to tell you, that Miss Lowell died two weeks ago.'

I sat down rather suddenly.

'Died?' I thought I must have misheard.

The man nodded and the woman hurried over to reception and returned with a paper cone of water from the cooler. I was surprised to notice that my hand shook as I took it from her.

'I don't understand.' I said. 'She was fine.' A terrible thought struck me. 'Was it the 'flu?'

The woman sat down beside me.

'She was involved in an auto accident. I'm so sorry for your loss.'

'What?' I really couldn't take it in. 'But she didn't drive.'

'No,' she hesitated, assessing what my reaction might be before continuing, 'she was hit by a – by a cable car.'

'Whilst crossing against the lights.' The man added.

The woman shot him a look. She seemed to realise that it might sound like Cassie deserved it, so she added:

'Her funeral is today. I can give you the details, if you'd like them?'

Which neatly controlled the situation and got me heading to the door before I could do anything embarrassing like burst into tears or hit the man.

The rain was beginning to come down with more force and it took me a while to get to the cemetery, unsurprisingly, as they weren't places I'd ever taken much interest in before. Even when I'd found the right place, locating where her actual interment was happening took even longer. I arrived at the graveside, cold and very wet, and late. I was clutching some sad and wilted flowers I'd paid a fortune for at the cemetery gates. I satisfied myself that I was finally at the right graveside by checking the single floral tribute that was made up of plastic flowers and a card that simply read RIP Cassie Lowell and looked as though it was a re-usable wreath provided by the funeral home and had seen service many times before. I had got there just as the brief service was ending and the coffin was being lowered into the ground. I looked at my fellow mourners; there were two men, both looking uncomfortable. One was a skinny, miserable excuse of a man who, when he saw me looking at him, pulled his cap further over his eyes and stared at the ground. The other man was black, wearing a cheap mac over his dress shirt and trousers and holding a large black umbrella. He was also unmistakably a cop. I knew Cassie had no family to speak of, at least no one close, but I was surprised at so few friends and colleagues. Perhaps the weather and fear of catching the flu put people off any kind of public gathering, but even so, I would have expected some to have braved the weather to pay their respects. To say goodbye to Cassie. As I stared down at the simple casket, I thought about the waste that such a random accident could have happened to someone so young and vibrant. All those years I could have come to see her, could have persuaded her to love me, come away with me, marry me, and now it was too late. Once the cemetery staff withdrew, to allow us our final goodbyes, I threw my pathetic flowers into the grave and turned to leave. The skinny guy was already hurrying towards the exit, and I was torn between running after him and stopping to speak to the cop. As if seeing my indecision, the policeman stepped forward and made my mind up for me.

'Did you know Miss Lowell well?' He asked, polite

enough, for now.

'I did, once upon a time.' I told him. He was in his thirties, with an athlete's build and a nice face. The sort of face Cassie would have called homely. When she was being polite, that is.

'Not seen her recently?' We started walking towards the main path and he let me shelter a little under his umbrella as we did so. Like I say, he was nice.

'Moved away five years ago.'

'Been back in that time?'

I shook my head.

'But you did come back when you heard she had died.'

I shook my head again.

'I didn't know until I got here.' I explained. 'I'm a reporter, got sent out to cover the virus story and thought I'd look her up. The people at her workplace told me about the funeral.'

'You went there?'

'Yes. When I couldn't get hold of her. Just this morning. It was a real shock, I can tell you.'

He nodded and stopped. We'd got to his car.

'Where are you staying?' He asked me, 'Can I give you a lift?'

As the rain dripped down my collar, I gratefully accepted, even if it did mean he was going to ask me questions the whole way down town. There was information I was hoping to get out of him too.

In the event, he got a lot more information out of me than I did him. I guess the whole day, finding out that Cassie was dead and then going to her funeral, had knocked me off kilter, at least, that was my excuse to myself. I found out that his name was Detective

Kevin Carpenter, and what he did tell me, was that it was, to all intents and purposes, a pretty straight forward case. Cassie stepped out in front of a cable car and died instantly. It was a dark wet night and the gripper who was driving had seen nothing but a blur of movement to his right before the awful bump that told him he'd hit something. Only two witnesses had come forward: the man who was with her and another man who was apparently passing by at the time. Apparently, was the word the detective used. To all intents and purposes had been his phrase too. They seemed strange at the time and even more so when I looked back on the conversation. It was as though he was intimating that there was something suspicious about the accident, but I had no idea what. I assumed, as it happened at night and in the company of a man, that Cassie had been drinking, drunk even, but what I couldn't understand is why she'd been in that part of town so late at night. Perhaps the man who had been with her at the time could tell me. Detective Carpenter had told me that his name was Ed Davey and that he had been the other mourner at the graveside.

It didn't take a mastermind to work out that Carpenter thought there was something funny going on with Cassie's death and by the time he dropped me outside my hotel, I had made the decision to trace Ed Davey and ask him what had really happened when she died, and I had the feeling that that was exactly what Carpenter wanted me to do.

After the night before, I had good reason to steer clear of all the usual bars frequented by news men; I really wanted to avoid bumping into Martin again. I'd already said too much and aroused his suspicions, besides I wanted to track down Cassie's friend and her only mourner, Ed Davey. I phoned in a brief report, describing the drug distribution centre and hoped my editor was impressed that I was at least trying to get a different angle, even if I had nothing of real interest to put in the piece. A cursory internet search had thrown up about forty Edward Davey's and that was before I had even tried variations on that name, but one immediately caught my eye. He lived about a couple of blocks from Cassie's apartment, away from the park, and sharply down the desirability league. It seemed as good a place as any to start.

I had no luck finding Davey at his place so I walked around the area, going into all the bars and diners I came across and finally struck lucky in a bar that was at least half a step up from my choice of the night before judging by the number of people there if not the cleanliness. Davey was hunched over an empty beer glass and looking pretty sorry for himself. He nearly rabbited when I sat down next to him, but I kept a firm hand on his arm, assuring him I meant him no harm and offered to buy him a drink. He looked over his shoulder, checking out the clientele, the small number of other customers were all busy watching the game on a TV that had seen better days, like the bar itself. No one was paying us any attention. Reassured, he nodded his acceptance and I signalled the bartender.

'I'm an old friend of Cassie's.' I said by way of introduction once I'd ordered beers for us both. I decided against whiskey chasers this time around to give my liver a break.

'Me too,' he sucked hungrily at the beer as soon as it was set in front of him, almost draining the glass in one gulp. I waved and pointed and another appeared, and he set on that as fast. I hoped he was going to slow down sometime soon or I was going to need more cash.

'Where'd you meet?'

He shrugged.

'Around.'

'Around where?' I persisted. I just couldn't see why Cassie would ever be with a loser like him.

'Here.' He said, looking round again. 'And other places.'

'Bars, you mean?' I was beginning to understand as he nodded. Perhaps Cassie had taken up alcohol, well, taken it up in a bigger way than she had when we were together. She had always liked a drink and we had got drunk together on many an occasion. Perhaps, like with me, things had gotten worse. Perhaps she had begun drinking so heavily that she hung around bars like this, picking up men like Ed. It was a depressing thought and maybe a small look into my own future as a sad, lonely drunk.

'Were you with her when she died?' I asked and I could see it crossed his mind to deny it, but he had seen me talking to the detective so he had to assume I knew he was, and he finally nodded.

'What exactly happened?' I asked as the third beer was slammed down on the bar in front of him, well the third since I had arrived, anyway. Chances were he'd had more than a couple before that. He hesitated before sipping his drink this time, giving himself time to think about answering the question, but whatever the reason, I was glad he hadn't downed it in one again.

'How'd you mean?' He parried.

'I mean, how come she got run down by a cable car the other side of town? Was she drunk?'

'I wouldn't say she was drunk, exactly. I mean, we'd been out, had a few, but…' He left it hanging there, letting me get the picture. They'd been on a bar crawl. We used to do that sometimes, me and Cassie, getting drinks in different bars and running out. Cassie liked to see how often we could get away without paying, said it added excitement to the night. I disagreed about that, it used to scare me shitless. I could imagine how my parents would feel if they ever got to know, or if I got arrested. They would never have understood why we did it. To be honest, I didn't understand either. It wasn't my kind of excitement.

I felt an overwhelming sadness at the picture I now had of Cassie: the neighbourhood drunk. How could it have happened? I had been so busy messing up my life, working too hard, drinking too much and having one meaningless physical relationship after another as I tried to forget her, was it possible that she had been doing the same? If I'd stayed around, kept in touch, could I have stopped it all from happening? I shook my head. I was probably making myself more important to Cassie than I had ever been in reality. If she had decided to become an alcoholic, even a functioning alcoholic, there was nothing I could have done to stop her had I been there. I had never managed to stop her from doing anything she wanted to do.

I paid the tab and was turning to leave when another thought occurred to me.

'Do you know the name of the other guy?'

'Other guy?' Ed looked completely blank.

'Who stopped to help after the accident?' I clarified.

'What?' He looked panicked. 'No. You're mistaken. There was no one else there.' And he almost ran out of the bar in his effort to get away from me and my questions. Or maybe he had just realised that having seen me pay the tab, the free beer was no longer on offer. I hurried after him, but there was a squeal of brakes and I saw him running across the road, only just reaching the other side without being hit himself. I didn't go after him; I had no desire to meet with Cassie's fate, even if Ed seemed set on it. Besides I had a lot of thinking to do. I did what I always do when I need to think things through, despite the persistent drizzle, I walked. I walked through Pacific Heights, turned south at Precidio and through the Panhandle and then on to Golden Gate Park. I thought I was just walking, but my legs, or my subconscious, was guiding me, and then I was there, on Hippie Hill again. I was alone, but I didn't try to get out of the rain by sheltering under the trees. I remembered a day soon after I first met Cassie when we had gone for a walk in Golden Gate Park and ended up on the hill. The sun had been shining that day, unlike now. We had laid down on the grass and she'd told me that she'd come to San Francisco because her dad had always sung the Scott Mackenzie song to her when she was little. A sort of lullaby. She'd been fascinated by the song, the picture of people with flowers in their hair, the whole hippie story. When her father died and left her an orphan with a small inheritance, she'd decided to go to the place he had never made it to, but sang about, and applied to the State University. When she told me this story, I confessed that I didn't know the song and so she sang it to me, the whole way through. She knew all the words perfectly, and her voice was just so beautiful. As someone who cannot hold a tune for the life of me, I was in awe. And as she sang, she picked daisies and made a chain which she placed, like a crown, around my head. Very much in the spirit of the song and of Hippie Hill itself. Later that evening, we made love for the first time and I think that was the day I truly fell in love with her. The song became our secret code, she had only to hum a few lines for me to know that she was thinking of me, that she wanted me and I would move heaven and earth to find a way to be alone with her, alone so that we could make love again. I may have cried that night as I stood on Hippie Hill and remembered the good times with Cassie, it was hard to tell with all the rain running down my face.

Later that night, how much later I have no idea, I only know I was wet to the skin as I walked around the area where Cassie had died, trying to make sense of what Carpenter said had happened to her and thinking about the times we had spent together. The place where the accident had happened made little sense to me. It wasn't a place you would choose to go to without a reason, it wasn't a residential area and it wasn't on the way to anywhere Cassie would likely visit. It was completely deserted at this time of night, all the businesses around were closed. No one would have been around the night Cassie was killed either I reckoned and I was surprised there had been any witnesses to what happened at all. The rain had finally stopped but the damp sea air had caused a fog to settle over the city, muffling sound and blurring vision. I was deep in my thoughts, taking little notice of what was going on around me, when I stepped off the kerb and was brought rapidly back to my senses by a blast from a horn. I jumped back as a cab drove past me, driver gesticulating angrily and pointing at the 'Don't Walk' sign. I stood for a moment or two collecting myself. I had so nearly gone the same way as Cassie. It seemed ironic. I took a deep breath and steadied myself and that was when I heard it. Someone humming the opening line of 'If you're going to San Francisco.' And not just anyone humming it, it sounded just like Cassie. I turned around, checking for people on the sidewalk behind me, but there were none. In front of me, a cable car had stopped at the red light. And that's when, as the lights changed again, I swear I saw her, in the cable car. She was looking away from me, but I would have known the back of her head, her hair, her beautiful chestnut hair falling in waves to her shoulders and the way she held herself, anywhere.

'Cassie!' I shouted, and in that instant, the lights changed and as the cable car jerked forward again, she turned to the sound of my voice, eye's widening in surprise. I couldn't see if she called my name, or smiled, as the lower part of her face was covered by a mask, but I knew it was her. I ran after the cable car, trying to dodge the traffic, but it quickly disappeared into the swirling fog and I stopped and shook my head to clear it. It couldn't have been Cassie I told myself over and over again. I thought it was my mind playing tricks on me, because I'd been thinking of her, and eventually I stopped at a warm and friendly looking bar, where the bartender lent me a towel to dry myself a little and didn't object to the drips I left beneath my barstool. I had a few drinks as I convinced myself I had seen her, and then a few more to convince myself I had not.

Next day, head hurting, and my mind foggier than the weather of the night before, I filed more copy, with more horrifying mortality statistics and still no answer as to why so many people were dying from Influenza in and around Northern California. The health department were beginning to sound defensive and insisted that they were following the exact same protocol on who should get the drug as other parts of the country. *Zeroflu* was in such short supply everywhere that a list of priority people had been drawn up. Pregnant women were considered to be amongst those most at risk, because of their reduced immune response, closely followed by children, the sick and the elderly. There was enough of the anti-viral medication for it to be available to all of them, but not to those of us who had none of these risk increasing factors. As the health authorities, and the company repeatedly explained, there was a shortage because the drug companies, and the people whose job it was to predict what new diseases would appear, had all been caught on the hop by this virus, an unexpected mutation from an earlier type of bird flu. The company was ramping up production as fast as it could, and, of course, they were repeatedly being asked to release the patent so that other companies could join them in manufacturing it, but everyone knew that the pandemic would be over before anyone else could get their production lines up and running. The drug company was in a no-win situation. Even so, I am sure they would do it after a few more televised interviews with the weeping parents of angelic dead toddlers, if only to show that they were doing everything in their power to help save lives. There was also a statement from the company, confirming that they were supplying exactly the same drug to every part of the country from their distribution centre in Oakland, which struck me as strange. Why would they feel the need to say that?

Duty done, I was finally ready to go over what I had seen and heard the night before. What I thought I had seen and heard. I had been thinking of Cassie, of her singing San Francisco in the park, visiting the place where she first sang it to me. It was a foggy, eerie night and I had been drinking. A lot. Then, a snatch of the tune hummed by a woman. A woman on a cable car, wearing a mask. Was I sure it was her? Was I even sure I had heard someone humming the song? It could have been in my head. In the cold light of morning it didn't seem to amount to much more than an over active imagination, but I couldn't completely dismiss it. I wasn't generally given to imagining things, even when I was drunk. I was more likely to forget stuff than make it up and the memory of her still nagged away at me, much as I tried to dismiss it. That's why, with all my questions about Cassie's death, I thought I'd take a look at the official version of what actually happened on the night she died. I checked local news reports online and found a reference to the accident and the hospital where she was taken. There was also a short piece on the inquest and in that report the cause of death was given as accidental, with the coroner remarking on the dangers of walking at night having consumed alcohol. I could vouch for that. There was no mention of anyone else at the scene, but also no suggestion of anything odd about the accident. I had little hope that the full inquest and autopsy reports would be publicly available yet, with the number of people dying of flu, it might well take months. From experience, I knew that getting medical records from the hospital required a lot of developing relationships and heavy-duty bribery, but the morgue was a much simpler place to get information. Somehow the fact that their clients were dead made people worry less about revealing their most intimate secrets.

True to form, I was able to find a technician who, for a comparatively small consideration, gave me a copy of Cassie's full autopsy report. I tucked it in my pocket and went to find a coffee shop where I could top up on caffeine and read the file in peace. The pictures were too brutal to look at and I skipped to the summary at the end. Cause of death seemed pretty clear, she had massive injuries to her head and body and her blood alcohol level was through the roof, supporting the theory that she was drunk at the time of the accident. There were also traces of a variety of other drugs, including a large amount of cocaine. It wasn't any of these facts that were so surprising, but when I went through the report more thoroughly, it was some of the incidental findings that aroused my suspicions. Her jaw had been smashed but the condition of the few teeth left and the state of her gums suggested long-term, poor dental hygiene which, along with acute periorificial dermatitis, were attributed to drug use. I had to look up perioral dermatitis, it was described as an inflammatory rash around the mouth and nose. Everyone knew tweekers had bad teeth and facial skin sores, but Cassie wouldn't use crystal meth, I was sure. She wasn't a saint where drugs were concerned, she smoked weed occasionally and she had the odd line of coke when I knew her, but this was different, this report suggested she had become a habitual amphetamine user. I couldn't believe it. Frustrated, I went back to the beginning. The pictures were unrecognisable. Her face was obliterated and I couldn't bear to look too closely at them, so I moved on to read the general information in the introduction to the report. The overall details of how the body looked before they cut her up. An under-nourished body of a Caucasian female, brown hair, brown eyes, approximately five foot six and less than a hundred pounds. Much lighter than when I knew her, but nothing to say it couldn't be Cassie. Then, under distinguishing marks, there were several tattoos that she hadn't had when I knew her, but more importantly, there was no mention of the one I knew her to have, a small red rose on the outside of her right ankle, and no mention of an appendix scar. I went through the report again and steeled myself to examine the pictures properly. There didn't even seem to be anything where the tattoo should have been, not even a scar. I moved onto the detailed report. Listed under organs was an appendix. Cassie might have lost weight, she might have taken up tweeking, she might even have had her rose tattoo removed by an expert who didn't leave a scar, but I felt sure she couldn't have grown a new appendix. I had been there that night when her stomach bug got worse and was finally so bad I insisted something be done and took her to the emergency room. They said she was lucky I took her in when I did, that her appendix had been fit to burst. Cassie had called me her Savior, told everyone I had saved her life. I'm sure that wasn't true, but it made me proud all the same. I checked the name on the report, and the circumstances of death in case I had been given the wrong file, but no, it was definitely Cassie's. It was just that unless she had grown a new appendix, either the pathologist had messed up or the body they autopsied wasn't Cassie.

'It can't have been her!' I told Carpenter later. It had taken a while for me to get to see him, refusing to accept no for an answer every time they said it and I had resorted to shouting at one point, never a good thing to do in a police station as a general rule, but finally, my persistence paid off. I think he only agreed to speak to me because he was worried about what I might do if he didn't. Reporters aren't usually liked by cops, they tend to think we get in the way rather than help them, believing that the story is more important than justice, and they are probably right. Carpenter seemed distracted, he'd been the one to sow the seeds of doubt about Cassie's death in my mind, but now he seemed barely interested. I told him about the autopsy report, which made him raise an eyebrow, he was probably making a mental note to tell the mortuary director he had a bent tech, but I carried on anyway. He wasn't overly convinced by the missing tattoo but the appendix had him listening I thought.

'Who identified the body?' I asked.

'The boyfriend.' He told me.

'And who said he was her boyfriend?' We both knew the answer to that. He did. The skinny guy. Ed Davey.

'Okay,' Carpenter leant forward, 'so maybe he

wasn't really her boyfriend, but he was the guy who was with her, and he saw what happened. It was an accident.'

'But it wasn't Cassie, so he must have lied.'

'Perhaps the pathologist made a mistake, I don't think them listing an appendix in with the other bits is enough to say it wasn't her. Do you have any idea how much pressure these guys are under? Just how many bodies they have to autopsy a day?'

It seemed that Carpenter wasn't yet convinced and I wasn't ready to tell him that I thought I had seen her and heard her, on a cable car. I wasn't totally convinced that I had really done so myself anyways, so I could hardly expect him to believe me.

'Why are you so sure it was an accident?' I asked him. 'I mean, you as good as told me you were suspicious about something.'

He looked up sharply, but didn't reply, which set me thinking.

'Did you say the driver, the gripper, saw anything suspicious?'

Carpenter shook his head.

'Nope. Nothing. His position was too far back.'

'And the passer-by? Did you check him out?'

Carpenter hesitated.

'He was a nobody, lived on the street.'

'And he didn't know either Davey or Cassie?' I persisted.

'Not that we could find out and he's gone now. Found dead.'

'Natural causes?'

'Fight over a bottle of vodka. He lost. It happens.' Carpenter sighed. 'Look, it just seemed convenient for her to die like that.'

'Convenient?'

'The timing.'

'And the death of the witness, too.'

He nodded.

'Never did find out what he was doing so far from his usual patch, or why Davey gave him the bottle of vodka he was killed over.'

'You know it was Davey that gave it to him?'

'Bought it the day before the accident, but didn't give it him until after.'

I was having difficulty taking in what he was saying, and even more so, what he was not saying.

'You were keeping tabs on Davey?' I asked. He didn't respond. 'And Cassie?'

He looked down, not wanting to catch my eye. I'd hit the nail on the head. For a moment, I couldn't believe it, but then I thought about some of the things we had done, that Cassie had done, when I knew her. She was reckless, a law unto herself. I could imagine her breaking the rules, the law even, but what was he suggesting?

'You think she was killed? Why?' It seemed ridiculous.

'Let's just say there were people who may have wanted her dead, and then,' he clicked his fingers, 'she was.'

I was about to ask more when we were interrupted by Carpenter's cell phone ringing. He checked to see who it was and held up a hand to stop me.

'Gotta take this.' He said and spoke into the phone.

'Hi.' He listened for a moment or two, concern etched all over his face. 'Okay, I'll be back as soon as I can.' He disconnected and wiped a hand across his forehead. He was a troubled man.

'Look, I can't tell you not to look into this.' He

told me. 'But I have to warn you to be careful. Your ex was into some pretty heavy-duty people, these guys don't mess around.' He ushered me to the door, all business, in a hurry.

'You've got her wrong.' I tried to tell him, but he wasn't listening and closed the door firmly in my face before I had the chance to ask him more. It seemed clear to me that whatever else, he didn't think Cassie's death was an accident, even if he didn't believe me that she hadn't died. Looking at the closed office door, there was something else I learned, Carpenter wasn't a homicide detective, he was in the gangs and narcotics division. I should have told him about the Mexicans tossing Cassie's apartment, but somehow, I wasn't sure I wanted to just yet, I was already regretting telling him that I didn't think she was dead, even if he didn't believe me.

My head was buzzing when I left the detective's office. It seemed clear to me that Carpenter was investigating Cassie before her apparent death, and although he suspected that it might not be an accident, he did think she was dead. He had warned me that she was in with some pretty bad guys, therefore, he suspected that she'd been killed. The fact that he was a gangs and narcotics detective made me think this was a drug related investigation, no prize for my deduction there. And Cassie worked for a pharmaceutical company. Could she have been supplying a gang with prescription opioids direct from the company? Maybe she was about to talk and he thought they had killed her to shut her up. She might even have stumbled on something accidentally and not been involved herself. I wanted her to be innocent, you see, you can probably tell.

The bar I had inevitably hurried to as soon as I left Carpenter, had a television high up on the wall, showing highlights of various sporting events from the night before. Being so close to the precinct, it was busier than most, with cops just off duty, wannabee cops and cop groupies all hanging out together and drinking. One look at me and they could tell I was not one of them and I was left to drink in peace. Relative peace, that is. My thoughts were in turmoil as I tried to work out just what was going on. Could Cassie have gotten involved in drugs and gangs? It didn't seem likely, but then, I hadn't seen or spoken to her in recent months, years even, and a lot could have changed in that time. I was going backwards and forwards over the possibilities when, during a break from sport, the news came on the TV. The anchor was saying something about the flu epidemic, a look of concern on his face, and then cut to a reporter standing in front of a hospital emergency entrance. I turned slightly on my bar stool to listen to the news report.

'That's right Doug. I'm here at the Children's Hospital in San Francisco, where this morning, tragically, five year old Tommy Durrance lost his fight for life. Mr and Mrs Durrance have praised the efforts of the medical staff to save Tommy but say they were told it was just too late and the boy was too sick.'

The bartender switched the television over to another sports channel, dead children weren't going to attract customers, I guess, although it certainly made me want to drink more. My thoughts turned to the reason I was in San Francisco, besides wanting to see Cassie, that is. I felt guilty that I hadn't managed to find any grieving relatives to interview and knew I would only be given a certain amount of leeway with my hints at sources in the pharmaceutical company if I didn't come up with something that might interest the paper's readers. The beast needed constant feeding as my editor was always telling me, when he could bring himself to speak to me at all that is. The need for more and more copy in this day and age of digital news tended to lead to lots of unsupported speculation and if I didn't come up with at least a few facts to fill up the space, I was going to have to explain to my editor exactly why he should carry on paying me. Let alone pay any expenses. With that in mind, I spent the afternoon, dutifully trawling hospitals, finding weeping and anxious relatives and putting together some sob stories to keep the beast happy.

I was coming out of the general hospital when I saw Carpenter. He was helping a petite, black woman into a car with a solicitude that told me this was someone dear to him. She looked unwell, clammy, tired, dressed in baggy sweats and holding a handkerchief to her mouth, and as she sank back into the passenger seat, she closed her eyes. Carpenter hurried round to the other side of the car and got in, reaching across to do up her seat belt before driving away.It occurred to me that the woman might be his wife, or his sister, and that she was the cause of his earlier pre-occupation and his pushing me out the door. If she had the flu, I could understand that.

I needed to talk to other news hounds, and pick up what their theories were, so I braved the bar at the Four Seasons. It was no use going to the one in my own hotel as no serious papers would, or had, put their reporters there. Hotel bars, in general, are not my kind of place to drink, too quiet, too luxurious, too pricey. The bar at the Four Seasons was as highly polished as you would expect: glass, marble, leather and wood; it all shone, but the bar wasn't quiet. It was loud and busy, everyone talking at once. I could see that even the terrace was full. I didn't imagine half the journalists in the room were actually staying at the hotel, but judging by the number of people demanding receipts, they were all intent on charging their drinking to their employers. Good luck with that, I thought, knowing that there was no way I'd get away with doing it, but then, I was with a small provincial paper and my name was mud, so perhaps I wasn't the best judge.

The buzz in the room seemed to be centering on the pharmaceutical company and its processes, with theories of a substandard batch being bandied about. It made sense and given my boast of having a source in the company, it was no great surprise when I saw Martin shouldering his way through the crowd towards me. I looked behind me to see if there was an escape route, but there was nothing but walls, of people as well as the walls of the room. The only way out was directly past Martin. He had me cornered and he knew it.

'Joe! Let me get you a drink.' He pushed his way to the bar and waved at the barman. Martin must've already bribed the man because he dropped what he was doing and hurried over. Martin ordered a large bourbon for himself and looked at me, challenging me to refuse.

'Same.' I capitulated and took the proffered glass.

'Where'd you disappear to? I was beginning to think you were avoiding me.'He said and smiled to show that he knew that was exactly what I had been doing and he didn't blame me for it. 'Did you manage to meet up with your contact?' He added with feigned nonchalance as we moved to a slightly quieter area away from the bar. I drank my bourbon and thought about lying.

'She died.' I told him. That was the official story, after all. It seems strange but I think that it was really only then, in the bar as I talked to Martin, that the possibility of Cassie being dead, even if she wasn't the corpse they'd autopsied, filled my mind and then, dead or not, the probability of my never seeing her again, finally hit home and a feeling of despair overwhelmed me.

Martin gave me a look that said he thought I was making it up.

'The mysterious Mexican's get her?' He sneered and then laughed, and a thought occurred to me. 'Honestly Joe, you're going to have to do better than that.' He said with a shake of his head. Which was when I punched him. It felt good. I'd been wanting to hit someone for a few days and it was a relief to finally do it.

The rest of the evening passed in a bit of a haze. I'd been pulled off Martin before I could do any serious damage to anywhere other than his nose and he'd insisted he needed to go to the hospital. I do remember him shouting that he'd sue my ass off and make sure I never worked for a paper again and I seem to remember saying I hoped he caught flu in the emergency room, which I was pleased to see gave him pause for thought. I heard later he had decided discretion was the better part of valor and he'd nursed his bloody nose himself. Hospitals were dangerous places in these times, particularly ones in San Francisco. I also remember getting clapped on the back by a number of my colleagues all saying that they'd wanted to do something similar to Martin themselves over the years, and I got bought a lot more bourbon, my last one having been spilled when I hit the man.

I woke up late the next morning with a sandpaper tongue and a head ache to end all headaches. I vaguely remembered hitting Martin and groaned. Why had I been so stupid? I needed coffee, gallons of coffee, before I was going to be able to go over last night's events and try and make any sense out of them. And even then, I was pretty sure my actions would still seem crazy. Martin wasn't the type to forget something like getting sucker punched in a room full of his peers in a hurry.

I looked at my phone, there were lots of missed calls and messages, most from my editor which I ignored. I did not feel strong enough for a balling out, or worse. If he'd been looking for an excuse to fire me before, I'd handed him one on a plate. In amongst all the messages there was one from Carpenter, saying he wanted to speak to me. He didn't mention assault charges and if Martin hadn't called the cops last night, I didn't think he would have done so this morning, he was much more likely to have made a complaint direct to the paper and besides, Carpenter was with the gang division, he wouldn't be interested in a little spat between journalists, would he?

Carpenter was out when I rang, but I left him a message before deleting the rest of the voicemails and texts. I really didn't want to know whether I had a job or not. Finding out what had happened to Cassie was my priority. My only priority.

What had occurred to me just before I hit Martin the night before, was that my theory of Cassie having been innocent and killed by the Mexicans to shut her up, didn't hold water. They wouldn't still be around, if that was what had happened. They were looking for something when I saw them in her apartment. Drugs? Money? Cassie herself? I had no idea and the only person I knew, other than Carpenter, who might have that information, was Ed Davey. Because, if Cassie was alive, and I was becoming more and more convinced that she was, he was the only person who would know what happened that night now that the other witness was conveniently dead. Only person other than Cassie, that is, because I had come to the conclusion that she had enlisted them to fake her own death. It was a very Cassie style answer to a problem. I didn't know why the cops and the Mexicans all seemed to be after her, but I could easily believe she might think that being dead was a good way out. Supposedly dead, that is. As an answer to staying out of prison, and alive, it was neat. I gave her that. The lady in the morgue instead of her, probably wouldn't though, and I sincerely hoped she had been dead before she was thrown under the cable car. Somehow, I didn't want to think too much about that.

Davey was smart enough not to be in the bar I had found him in before, but not smart enough to keep away from bars altogether or at least leave the area. The smell of beer as I entered the place almost made me gag, so I wasn't unhappy that he immediately rabbited when he saw me. He was easy to catch and drag into a diner further up the road. I dumped him in a seat and signalled to the waitress who came over with cups and the all-important coffee pot. Davey looked anxiously round, before hunching down in his seat and pulling his cap further over his face. This was a man who definitely did not want to be seen talking to me.

'I need to know about the night Cassie supposedly died.' I said, straight to the point. My headache was too bad and my brain too foggy for me to do anything else.

'I don't know any-,' my words suddenly sank in and he stopped. 'What do you mean supposedly?'

'I know she didn't die that night.' Okay, so I didn't know exactly, but I was pretty sure.

There was a pause.

'That's stupid.' He said finally, but he wasn't a very convincing actor.

'I've read the autopsy report, and whoever the poor tweeker was who fell under the bus, it wasn't Cassie.'

He fiddled with his cup, swirling the coffee round, trying to think what he should tell me. I lost patience.

'Look, just tell Cassie that I need to speak to her, okay? That I won't let up until I've found her. She knows that and she knows how to contact me.' I stood up and tossed a few dollars on the table before leaving. From down the street, I could see him on the phone, looking agitated as he talked to whoever it was on the other end. My money was on it being Cassie. At least I hoped it was her and not the Mexicans. Once the call was finished, Davey hurried away and disappeared into the crowd. I could just make out his funny stooping walk as I followed, but then a man cut in front of me, almost pushing me over. I staggered and bumped into a person coming out of a shop doorway. By the time I had apologised, both Davey and the man who had knocked into me had gone. I thought about chasing after them both but changed my mind, something about the way the man had shouldered me out of the way was very deliberate and reminded me of the man I had seen at Cassie's apartment, not the little one at the door, but the tank of a man chucking her belongings around.Besides, I really didn't have the energy for chasing after anyone anymore. I had to trust that Davey could look after himself and that he had let Cassie know my request already and that she would agree to meet me. I needed to know what was going on and I needed to see her again.

Meanwhile, there was a message for me from Carpenter, amongst yet more from my editor that I chose to ignore. The detective had agreed to meet me at the hospital. The meeting was set for eleven o'clock in the coffee bar. That was good. More coffee was definitely a good idea.

As I nursed my coffee and tentatively chewed a mouthful of donut while waiting for Carpenter, I listened to the latest voicemail from my editor. A video of me hitting Martin had gone viral, apparently. That's what comes of doing something stupid in front of dozens of reporters. Far from being grateful for all the free publicity, my editor had decided to fire me. Something about the reputation of the company but more likely about not wanting to get sued.

This trip was going from bad to worse but I didn't have time to dwell on it because Carpenter arrived at that moment, and if I thought my day was bad, it looked as if his was way worse.

He slumped at the table.

'Coffee?' I suggested.

He shook his head.

'I've had too much already.' He certainly looked like a man who had been up all night drinking coffee. He gave me a long look before continuing. 'You are pretty sure that your ex isn't dead, aren't you?'

'Yes.' I really didn't want to admit to my belief that I had seen her, and heard her, but somehow, that's exactly what I ended up doing. When I finished telling him, he sighed and rubbed his unshaven face.

'It figures. I thought her being dead was too good to be true.'

This seemed a little harsh.

'Why? What has she done to make you want her dead?'

Maybe I shouldn't have asked, but I did, and what he told me, horrified me.

He put an empty pill packet in front of me. I recognised the distinctive packaging. It was *Zeroflu*. He explained again that it was the only effective treatment for the flu, that it was made by the firm Cassie had worked for and it was in short supply. I knew all that. Then he put a second empty packet in front of me.

'Take a look at these and tell me if you can see any differences between them.

I looked at them, checked dates and batch numbers, printing, everything was identical and I told Carpenter that they were the same.

'And yet, they came from different cartons. They should be different batches. Have different numbers.'

I tried to think of a reason why that might have happened, but I couldn't. Maybe it was the hangover stopping me from working it out. I always think of simple human error before conspiracy and I suggested as much. Carpenter nodded.

'I agree, but it can't be an innocent mistake. There's just no way it could happen. We think someone in the Oakland distribution centre has been swopping out batches of the real medication for fake packets brought in from Mexico, and that's how the mistake occurred.'

'Why would they do that?' I asked, before realising that this was a stupid question. Anything in short supply means that people will pay over the odds for it. It's how black markets work and Carpenter confirmed as much.

'It started with just a few but they've upped the number recently and the wrong boxes got exchanged, so two cartons ended up with the same batch number. It's been our first and only break in the case. In finding the reason why the treatment doesn't seem to be working here in north California.'

His theory certainly fit the facts. I knew that the high cost of prescription medication in the US had led to a new traffic in drugs from Mexico, legal drugs, particularly insulin and heart medications. There was a high return on them and the risk of smuggling these medications was much less than bringing in illegal drugs, all the traffickers got was a fine and a slapped wrist if they were caught and it was a growing trade. Once the cartels got involved, they realised that they could make even more money if they didn't even bother to buy or make the drugs. If they were fake, nothing but sugar pills or water in a vial, all they had to do was copy the packaging. Sure, they'd kill off their customers, but who cared? That meant fewer witnesses and there were always plenty more where they came from. With the shortage of *Zeroflu*, it must have seemed easy picking to make their own fake treatment and con the worried rich into buying it, but it was an act of genius to exchange their sugar pills for the real deal and sell that to the highest bidder. A genius must have thought of that, but an evil genius, and I just hoped that person wasn't Cassie.

'How much has been changed?' I asked.

'That's just it, we don't know.' Carpenter said, in a voice gritty from exhaustion. 'A pack from every batch is being sent for testing, but by the time the results get back, all of it will already have been given out to patients. It's pretty easy to spot who got the real treatment and who got the fakes by then too, because the people who got the fakes are usually dead.'

I thought about the woman I had seen with Carpenter and wondered if she was dead too. Then I thought about Cassie. How could she do it? Because I had no doubt now that Cassie had been the person who, even if she hadn't physically exchanged the cartons, had made it happen.

'What made her run?' I finally asked and Carpenter shrugged.

'She must've realised we were getting close.'

I was desperately hoping she had been pressured into doing this terrible thing and had run because she couldn't bring herself to do it anymore, rather than that. The thought of those kids dying because of her was just horrific. And then I looked at Carpenter and saw just how personal this was for him.

'How is your wife?' I asked, sure that was who it had to be.

'Not responding to treatment.' He said and left me to go back and sit by her bedside. No wonder he hated Cassie. I was beginning to hate her myself.

I went back to my hotel to be handed my suitcase by reception instead of the key. It seemed the paper had been in touch and cancelled my room. The girl behind the reception desk did at least have the good grace to apologise for the inconvenience. I suspected that the company credit card would have been stopped as well. At least my cell phone was still working. I checked.

Any normal person would have rung up and begged for their job back, or maybe even bought themselves a flight back home at this point, but I didn't. I knew I had to find out what was happening and hear from Cassie herself why she had done something so terrible. I felt sure there had to be a reason and, hopefully, a good reason for it. I'd like to say that it never occurred to me that I was onto a great story, but that would be a lie. I knew that my only way back into the world of journalism was to get an exclusive and explosive piece, and maybe sell it to one of the big-name papers, like The New York Times, or maybe even a TV station, and then write a book about it. Nothing else would do. Nothing else would reinstate me in the eyes of the journalism world, well, those in authority anyway, I was probably something of a legend amongst the reporters who witnessed me hit Martin, but they weren't going to give me Job. Besides which, I didn't have enough money for the air fare to the place I had called home for the last few years if my company credit card had been stopped, my personal ones were all maxed out. There wasn't much leeway in my checking account either. Somehow, I hadn't planned on being unemployed. They say most of us are only three months away from being on the streets, I wasn't sure I was even that.

My most pressing problem was somewhere to stay. Somewhere free. I really didn't want to sleep rough on the street, or even at the bus station if I could help it and it really wasn't a big jump mentally to decide to go to Cassie's apartment. I mean, it's not like she was using it herself, right?

I got to her building and managed to get someone to buzz me in as before. In fact, it was quicker, perhaps they were getting used to people without keys demanding entrance. They really ought to have known better.

Cassie's apartment was the last on the landing and when I got there, I could see that the door was open. Not wide open, but an inch or two. I hesitated, I'd be lying if I said I wasn't scared, but the apartment felt empty and I hoped I was right and no one was waiting inside. I pulled off my jacket and used it to cover my hand before pushing the door open.

The room was as messy as I remembered from my last visit. That figured, I didn't expect the Mexicans to have cleared up after themselves, but I also didn't think they would leave the door ajar, would they? Not unless they wanted someone to come into the place and find -

Ed Davey was on the floor in the living area, lying in a pool of blood. You didn't have to be a doctor to know that he was dead. No one could live with that much of their head missing. Perhaps I should have found a way to warn Davey that he was being followed that night from the bar, but it was too late for recriminations now. As I looked at the bloody mess he had become, I thought about why he had been left there, in the apartment, with the door ajar, for anyone to find, or, more likely, for someone specific to find. The way he had been left was clearly a message, but was that message for me or for Cassie? Without waiting to find out I slid back out of her apartment and hurried along the landing towards the stairs. The last thing I needed was to be caught in someone else's home, with a dead body at my feet. Especially as I had been seen chasing said dead person out of a bar earlier.

As I got to the top of the stairs, I looked down and I could see a man waiting on the floor below, a big tank of a man, and he was waiting to stop anyone who was on their way down from the apartment, no doubt was in my mind. I was pretty sure it was the man who had been following Davey, back when he was alive. I jumped back and then froze. Had he seen me? I wasn't sure, but I also wasn't about to hang around to find out. I ran along the landing, looking for an exit but it was a small building and there was no second way down to the lobby. There was a probably a fire escape accessed from the rear of the apartments, I thought, but as it was, I was in a dead end.

A door opened and a woman came out with a bag of trash tied up ready to take to the chute. She looked up in surprise as I rushed towards her, pushed her back in to her hallway and clamped a hand over her mouth, kicking the front door shut with my foot. She looked terrified. Probably as terrified as I was. I heard footsteps on the landing and voices speaking Spanish. We stayed where we were, two people locked together and scared to all hell and back. The footsteps went away again, they were probably going to check if I was hiding in Cassie's place.

I looked at the poor woman whose home I had invaded.

'I'm really sorry, and I'm not going to hurt you.' I whispered. 'Those men you just heard? They were going to kill me, and if they find me here, they'll kill you too. Do you understand?'

She nodded.

'I'm going to remove my hand but if you scream, they'll hear and come back and kill us both, you do understand that, don't you?'

She nodded and I had to trust her. I knew I couldn't stay where I was for ever. We didn't have much time before they realised I wasn't in Cassie's place and came looking for me. They weren't stupid and would quickly work out that I must have gone into another apartment, so I had no choice but to hope the woman would be true to her word and not scream.

I let go of her and she looked at me, absolutely petrified, poor woman.

'Is there a back way out? A fire escape?' I asked her.

She nodded for a third time and pointed through her living room towards a door leading onto a balcony. I headed to it and unlocked it using the key she had left in the lock, in order to make a quick exit in case of fire or other emergency, I suppose. The door led onto a communal balcony for all the apartments on this floor which was served by a single metal fire escape. I looked left and right. The balcony was deserted. I quickly ran to the stairs and started down. I hadn't got more than a few steps down before I heard a shout.I looked up to see a man frantically trying to open the back door from Cassie's living room and shouting to his accomplice to come help. I jumped down several steps at a time. They might have seen me, but it took them valuable seconds to find the key to Cassie's exit, or rather not to find the key, as they kicked the door open and ran after me. I had a good lead and, all things considered, was confident I could get to the street before them. There was a metallic ping and a chip of paint flew off the hand rail. I realised they must be shooting at me, presumably with a silenced gun as I had heard no bang before the bullet hit the metal hand rail next to my hand. That was something I hadn't expected. Perhaps I should have done. I ran faster down the steps, almost tumbling down the last few and out onto the street. I wished the city wasn't so empty as I could have done with a crowd to hide in, as it was, I was in luck, a cable car was passing and I jumped on to the side ledge of the swaying car and clung onto a metal handle, just like they used to when the trams were first used. It is, however, strictly not allowed in these days of health and safety and I knew as soon as the driver saw me clinging to the side of the car, he would stop, so I prayed he wouldn't see me too quickly.

I nearly lost my grip as the cable car swung around the corner, but just about managed to hang on. I knew there was a stop up ahead, and I held on tight, clinging to the side, being cheered by some of the people on the tram and jeered by others. I didn't care what they thought of me, I was putting distance between me and the Mexicans. I jumped off as soon as the tram came to a halt and looked back as I ran up the hill. The tram driver was shaking his fist at me and shouting out that I was stupid, but the men chasing me were a long way off, still at the bottom of the hill and it took me no time at all to lose them in the shopping district. This was my town, and I knew my way around.

I soon found myself a noisy, crowded bar where people had gathered to remember a patron who had died of the flu that day. Far from being a quiet and sad affair, it looked like they were determined to send the man on his way with a riotous party and no one seemed to mind that I didn't know him. Everyone was welcome, so I quickly drank a beer to steady my nerves. Carpenter had warned me about the people Cassie was involved with, and he had been right. I just wished I'd been able to warn Davey too, but I am sure he already knew, which was why he had been so scared when I saw him in the bar. I went back over that meeting and whether I could have done anything different. We can all look back on our lives and see where we could have done better with hindsight, but I honestly don't think I could have warned him about the tail, particularly as I wasn't sure at the time if it was the cops or the bad guys who were following him. I was pretty sure I knew now.

I still had the problem of no one to turn to and no place to stay and I didn't want to spend too long in any one location in case they caught up with me, so in the end, I just walked around the city, stopping at random bars for beer at first, and later at all-night diners for coffee. All the time thinking about what I could do next, and how I had managed to screw up everything I'd ever wanted; Cassie, my career and quite possibly my life.I hoped Davey had managed to contact Cassie before he was killed, and that she in turn would get in touch with me, if she was still alive. I needed to know what was going on if I was going to get out of this alive myself. In the end, desperate for somewhere to sleep, somewhere warm, dry and safe, I went to the hospital and found myself a quiet corner with nothing but a hard, plastic chair to rest on. I sat down, leant against the wall and was instantly asleep.

I dreamt of Cassie, of that summer we spent together on Hippie Hill. I dreamt of making love to her, of running my hands through her hair and of her telling me that she loved me. That's how I knew it was a dream, because she never did say that to me in real life. Then there seemed to be someone shouting in the background, shaking my arm and I woke up to see Carpenter leaning over me. He didn't seem too pleased to see me.

'Hames! Hames!' he was saying loudly. 'Wake up, man! What are you doing here?'

I rubbed my eyes and looked around. This did not look like Hippie Hill. It took me a moment or two to remember that I had spent the night in the hospital.

'Man. You look like you need a coffee.' Carpenter said and it was on the tip of my tongue to say that he didn't look much better but I held back my retort. I really did need that coffee.

'So, tell me,' Carpenter said once we were seated in the hospital café with steaming mugs of insipid coffee in front of us. 'How come you're sleeping rough?'

I thought about that for a while. About if it was wise to be confiding in a policeman, whether or not he was on duty. On the whole, I decided, with no contact from Cassie, no job, nowhere to stay and a couple of Mexicans after me, I didn't have a whole lot to lose. So, I told him my story. Everything.

'Jesus!' Was his initial response. 'You are in a mess!' I couldn't disagree. To be frank, I didn't have the energy to do anything much at all. We sipped our coffee and after a while, he went and got more, along with a couple of pastries that looked and tasted stale, but were welcome all the same.

'Right.' He finally said and pulled a bunch of keys out of his pocket. He separated one out and handed it to me. 'Go to my place, get a shower, help yourself to something to eat and get some rest, you'll feel better for it.' He held up his hand as I started to object. 'Take it. I have to stay here for a while, but I'll be back in an hour or two and we can talk more then.'

Still I hesitated.

'You don't have much of a choice.' He said, and he was right. I had nowhere else to go so, I took the key and noted down the address and memorised the alarm code but I turned down the ten dollar bill he offered me for cab fare. A man has his pride, you know.

He was right about me feeling better once I had showered. There wasn't much food in the refrigerator, I was guessing that Mrs Carpenter hadn't been well enough to shop for a while and I finally settled on a bowl of Cheerios without milk. With more sugary food inside me, my brain even began to work and I felt guilty that I hadn't even asked Carpenter about his wife and how she was doing. There were little reminders of her around the whole house. A picture of the two of them on their wedding day was in pride of place on a shelf, there were notes stuck on the refrigerator, reminding about appointments made and to make, a shopping list on the side, and a copy of a sonogram, with the words: Baby Carpenter and a recent date on it. It was held in place by a heart-shaped magnet. I looked at it for a long time, trying to imagine how it must feel to watch your wife and unborn child die because of the greed of other people. People like Cassie. I was dog tired but it felt too intrusive to find a bed to sleep on in this house that so definitely wasn't mine, so I plugged my phone into charge, lay on the sofa and closed my eyes for a moment.

Next thing I knew, Carpenter was shaking me awake again and there was a smell of bacon in the air.

He'd made eggs, bacon and warm biscuits in the microwave and it tasted delicious. There was fresh coffee too and this time I remembered to ask after his wife, and the baby she was carrying.

'She's hanging on. They're hanging on.' Was all he would say and, 'I have to get back, soon.' I understood. Told him he didn't need to worry about me, but he said it was good to have something else to occupy his mind. To stop him thinking the worst. He told me he had called his precinct and got the latest on my escapades of the night before. Ed Davey's body had been found and my description was being circulated as a person of interest. The lady whose home I had invaded had given a surprisingly vague description of me, but I suppose shock blurs things a bit.

'Have you heard from your missing girlfriend?' he asked as he put a few things for his wife in a bag, a bed jacket, some toiletries, a fresh towel. I hoped she was well enough to appreciate them, perhaps he was hoping that too.

'No,' I told him, and it wasn't a lie, because I hadn't checked my phone, then. He told me to stay where I was. Not to go anywhere lest I get arrested, or killed by the cartel. He believed I wasn't responsible for Ed Davey's death, he told me, and that I didn't know where Cassie was, but he wanted me to let him know as soon as I heard from her, if I heard from her. If she knew Davey was dead, he didn't think it likely she'd risk getting in touch. He didn't say I was a jinx, but he implied it, and I couldn't argue with that. Davey would almost certainly be dead even if I hadn't contacted him, but I hadn't helped, that was for sure. Meanwhile, Carpenter's priority was his wife and child, and I understood that.

After he left, I cleared up the dishes for him, it was the least I could do given how good he had been to me, letting me stay in his place like it was some kind of safe house. Which it was, in a way. I switched on the TV, found a news channel and checked it for reports of a dead body and a home invasion. To my relief, my face wasn't plastered all over the tube, in fact, there was no mention of the incident at all. The news was full of death from a different cause: the flu. It was killing record numbers, with the frail elderly and pregnant women the biggest groups of victims, exactly the people the anti-viral drug was supposed to protect. I was beginning to get cabin fever after the third story of a mother dead and a family destroyed. I wondered if Carpenter was watching the same reports or if they kept away from news channels in the hospital. Unable to bear any more, I switched the TV off and reached for my phone. There was a message for me that had arrived whilst I was asleep. The number was unknown. My thumb hovered over the button. It might be from someone at the paper, warning me that the phone was being disconnected, or it might be from Martin's lawyers threatening to sue me, but somehow, I knew it was from Cassie. I held my breath as I touched the message icon on the screen.

'Fisherman's Wharf, 7pm.' The message said. That's it. No kiss or smiley face emoji, just a place and a time. It didn't need to be more precise, if it was Cassie, we had always met by the Fog Harbour Fish House, Pier 39, on the second level, where we could look down on the crowds below and people watch. She loved to do that, making up stories about them, where they came from, guessing what language the tourists were speaking, matching people up. 'Oh, they'd make a great couple. He's obviously a shy accountant and she'll bring him out of himself.' I often wondered if she would have matched us, if she had looked down and seen us making our separate ways along the wharf. I'm guessing not. No one would have.

It was mid-afternoon and I had plenty of time to get to the meeting place by seven. I thought about letting Carpenter know at once that she had been in touch, I honestly did, but then I thought I owed it to her to give her a chance to tell me how she had got caught up in all this before I got him and the police involved. I wanted her to convince me that it wasn't really her fault that these people were dying. I really didn't want to believe she was the sort of heartless bitch who could have done the things that Carpenter said she had and I felt I owed it to her to get her side of the story before I told him where to find her. If I told him where to find her, that is. And if the message wasn't from Cassie and it was the cartel setting up a meet with me, then I'd probably regret not having told Carpenter and having some back up in place, but it was a chance I was prepared to take, I thought. A little bit of me was still believing that when we met, I'd find out it was all some sort of horrible mistake and we would ride off into the sunset to live happily ever after together. That's just the sort of fool I was, I guess.

It's fair to say, I was pretty sure the message did come from Cassie. I didn't think the cartel knew who I was or what my phone number was or they would have contacted me before. But I wasn't a complete fool, before I went to the meeting, I intended to get my hands on a weapon. Now, California gun law is stricter than most and you can't just go into a gun shop and buy one, you have to have an up to date firearm safety certificate and even then, there has to be a ten day cooling off period before you can walk out the store armed to the teeth. I didn't have ten days. Or a firearm safety certificate for that matter. I checked out Carpenter's home. I thought he might have a gun lying around, either his service weapon, as he probably didn't need it in a hospital, or a spare, but I was dismayed to find a gun safe in his bedroom. If he'd left a gun at home, I wasn't going to be able to get my hands on it. Trust a cop to take gun safety seriously. I knew I could probably get myself a gun illegally, through a private sale, if I had time to get connected with criminals inside the city, or to travel into a more rural area where the gun laws would not be interpreted so strictly, but without much time and in downtown San Francisco, I was out of luck. Frustrated, I looked around in the kitchen and armed myself instead with a vicious looking paring knife. I just had to hope that was going to be enough and tried not to think of the ping of those bullets on the fire escape. Let's face it, if the cartel were waiting for me, me and my knife wouldn't stand a chance. As an afterthought, I left Carpenter a note and stuck it on the fridge, next to the sonogram.

It was six thirty when I arrived at Fisherman's Wharf. I'd read books where the hero decided to arrive early at potentially dangerous meets so that he would see if anyone unexpected arrived, like the Mexicans from the apartment perhaps. The trouble was, a thick sea fog had descended on the city so it was hard to see more than a few feet. To be fair, there weren't many people about either. I remembered the place always being packed with tourists, but the combination of fog and flu meant that I was pretty much on my own. Me, the bar keeps and wait staff and an occasional tourist, looking lost and forlorn. It was cold, damp and dispiriting, but I really didn't see anyone suspicious hanging around. I positioned myself in a dark corner of the balcony, half hidden behind an advertising board and watched and waited. It was freezing cold and I looked longingly at the open fire in the covered terrace bar, but it was too open for safety. I wanted to stay in the shadows.

I blew on my hands to warm them up, and felt in my pocket for the knife I had taken from Carpenter's kitchen. A man came up onto the balcony and I tensed. He was Asian, I thought, it was hard to tell as he was wearing a mask, and did nothing more than take a couple of photos and go straight back down the stairs, calling to his invisible family below and telling them there was nothing up there to see. He was right. I snuck a look at my watch and saw that it was five past seven and there was still no sign of Cassie. The cold, damp air was really seeping into my bones and it was a dulling sound as well, making it hard to tell where noises were coming from. I shivered and listened again. Was that footsteps I could hear? Somewhere in the distance there was the sound of angry voices and I was temporarily distracted, but it was just a domestic tiff. A girl who wanted more and a boy who thought she should be grateful for what she had. Then, there it was again. A definite footstep. Closer this time. On this level and behind me. I moved around the advertising hoarding to mask my position, but then she spoke.

'It's okay Joe, it's me.' And Cassie was there. Like me, she was one of the few people without a face mask on. But even if she had been wearing one, I'd have known her anywhere. A little older, a little thinner, but to me she still looked as good as she had done ten years ago, a lifetime ago, back before I was a burnt out, drunk, out of work hack, and I wanted to go back to that time again. I wanted her to take me back.

'It's good to see you.' She said and touched my arm.

'It's good to see you too.' I said, but I'm sure she already knew, my face said it all, in spades. She was dressed for the weather, and concealment, in a long raincoat with a hood and as a drop of wet cloud trickled down my neck, I wished I was too.

She led me away to a spot overlooking the harbour where people could sit and watch the ferries come in when the fog wasn't quite so dense.Needless to say, there was no one there now. We sat in silence for a minute or two, more to check for the sound of anyone following us than because we had nothing to say.

'How've you been doing, Joe?' she said at last.

'Oh, you know, pretty badly. How about you?'

She smiled.

'About the same.'

'Tell me what's going on.' I said and she sighed.

'You mean why is everybody after me?'

I nodded.

'All my plans, to be somebody, to have it all and what happened?' she looked at me. 'I ended up managing operations and assurance for a pharmaceutical company, that's what.' She gave a short laugh. 'Such a drag.' She looked at me. 'I'm guessing general dogsbody at a provincial paper wasn't what you had planned either.'

'Ex-general dogsbody,' I corrected her. 'I'm currently unemployed.'

'Sounds like you could do with a change of career.' I couldn't argue with that.

'She turned away from me, looked out across the harbour, what was visible anyway.

'A year or so ago, there was a glitch with one of the shipments of chemicals coming in to the company. The numbers didn't match, anyway, to cut a long story short, I found out that one of the warehouse men was facilitating illegal drug importation.'

'He was smuggling cocaine into the country through the company?'

'Yes, and he begged me to look the other way. Told me about his wife and family back home, frail mother, sick child, how they all relied on him.'

'He was Mexican?'

She nodded.

'And you turned a blind eye?'

She nodded again.

'I won't lie,' she still wasn't looking at me, 'the money was useful too.' She turned to see my reaction to her admission that her motives weren't entirely altruistic.

I shrugged. To be honest, it wasn't a surprise. She had never been a bleeding-heart liberal, money was important to her and I was pretty sure that was the bigger motive. Much bigger than a story about sick children and frail grandmothers which only a fool would believe.

Relieved to see that I wasn't shocked that she was paid by a cartel to help smuggle drugs, she continued her story.

'Then, when the flu began to take hold and tests showed that we were the only company with an effective anti-viral, and that there was going to be a massive shortage, the company went into overdrive. They really ramped up production, more and more chemicals and equipment were needed, supplies were going in and out of the warehouse and it was hard for anyone to keep track, it seemed like an ideal opportunity to increase our own operation.'

'But you didn't just smuggle illegal drugs in.'

'No.' She took a deep breath. 'At first I was asked to 'lose' a couple of boxes of *Zeroflu*, for use by the cartels, I was told. Then they wanted more. And more.' She turned to me. 'I knew they had to be selling it on the black market. Were probably getting a hundred, maybe a thousand, times the cost, because everyone wanted it. But that meant it was getting increasingly hard to cover the losses, so I suggested they give me something to replace the drugs with.'

'Make their own fake treatment.'

She nodded and continued.

'You've no idea how easy it was to replicate the packaging and the pills. They were already set up for it of course, they make all sorts of fake legal drugs to sell to people here who are too poor to buy the real thing and who don't have insurance. They could even fake the batch numbers in this case of course, because I could tell them what they were, and so that's how it started. We were in business. Me and a Mexican drug cartel.'

'Big business.'

'It turned out that way. You have to remember that we had no idea just how bad this flu was going to be at the beginning. It surprised everyone.'

'Then people started dying.'

'Yes. But I couldn't get out. It was too late. From the day I turned a blind eye to what was going on, they had a hold on me. I couldn't say no. You have to understand that, Joe.'

I knew she was right, but I couldn't help thinking she should have done it anyway.

She reached into her pocket and brought out two packets of *Zeroflu* tablets. I took them and examined them carefully. They looked identical to each other, and to the packet that Carpenter had shown me. She pointed to a small flaw in the printing of the expiry date where the letters exp had a smudged bit on the x.

'That's how we can tell the real from the fake.' She said. 'That little smudge there,' she pointed, 'means it's a fake.'

'Sounds like a pretty fool proof plan.' I told her, 'What went wrong?'

'Unfortunately, it was not completely fool proof.' She disagreed. 'The Cartel wanted me to exchange more and more of the drugs but I warned them about doing that. People were beginning to get suspicious.'

'People were dying.'

'And the authorities were beginning to notice that it was only happening in California.'

'Couldn't you have changed the cartons of drugs destined for other parts of the country, of the world even?'

She looked at me as if I was stupid.

'I wasn't that high up in the company. I only

controlled the shipments for California, interfering in other areas would have gotten me noticed much quicker.'

'So what did you do?'

'Told them they had to slow down. Stop even.'

'Why didn't they?'

She shrugged.

'They were making too much money. They wouldn't listen. Far from it. In fact, they wanted me to change more and more. I knew it was only a matter of time before somebody worked out what was going on. I had to get out.'

'You could have insisted or just stopped doing it.'

She shook her head.

'They wouldn't let me stop, Joe. You have to see that. They'd found a cash cow. Something even more profitable than smuggling cocaine, less risky too.'

'But just as dangerous for everyone else. More so, in fact.'

'People die all the time,' she seemed tired by it all, dismissive even.

'But you were helping them on their way. Sick children and frail grandmothers, exactly the people you said you started out trying to help.' It took her a moment to remember telling me the man she had started out helping had told her it was for his sick child and frail grandmother. It made me sure she had never for one minute believed they were real, or maybe she had made them up herself, to make me think better of her.

'That's why I got out. Disappeared. It was the only way to stop, just like you're saying I needed to and look where it's got me.' She gestured round, 'I'm alone. In hiding, pretending to be dead, for God's sake.'

That reminded me.

'And how exactly did you manage that?' I asked her. 'Where did you find someone who could be mistaken for you?'

She waved her hand dismissively.

'I left all that to Ed and his friend. They organised it. Pair of losers couldn't even get that right.'

I was horrified.

'They found some poor woman and threw her under a tram for you!'

'She was just some tweeker, for God's sake!'

'She was still a human being, Cassie! And Davey's dead now, his friend too.'

Her face hardened in response to my anger. If the news of their deaths was a surprise, she didn't show it.

'Like I said, they were losers.'

I shook my head.

'You need to come in.'

'You're joking. If the Cartel knew I was alive, they'd kill me just to make sure I couldn't talk about how they managed to do this and as a lesson to anyone else they ever work with.'

'I think they do know. They've been following me, I'm sure, and they killed Ed Davey and left him in your apartment, for you or me to find. They must suspect that you are still around otherwise they'd have gone, wouldn't they? Now that they know the games over? Why else would they hang around?'

She was much more concerned about the cartel knowing about her fake death than that Davey and his loser friend were dead. She glanced round nervously.

'Are you sure they didn't follow you here?'

'As sure as I can be.'

'And what about the police? Do they think I'm

dead?'

I shook my head.

'I told them I didn't think it was you they buried.'

'Jesus, Joe! What the hell were you thinking?' I could understand her anger, I wasn't sure why I'd told Carpenter either, except that, at the time, I thought it was right.

'I thought I was helping you, saving you from the cartel.'

She shook her head at that, and smiled, although the smile didn't reach her eyes.

'What a time to choose to come back into my life, Joe.'

'How was I supposed to know you had faked your own death. I thought there was something else going on.'

She thought for a moment.

'Maybe you're right.'

'About what?'

'About coming in.' She moved towards me and touched my sleeve. 'You could arrange it for me. Say I can give them the cartel, but I'll need their guarantee I'll get witness protection. And no prison. I want their word, not a day of prison time.'

I pulled away.

'Really?' I tried not to show how angry I was, 'You think they'd agree to that? What about all the people you've killed?

'What about them, Joe? I can't bring them back. Think of them as collateral damage, if you like, civilians killed in a war.'

'No, they weren't that, this wasn't a war, they died as a direct result of your greed.'

She winced at that, at my anger, perhaps, but I chose to believe it showed that she had a conscience.

'I'm sorry about them, of course I am, but they are not important here, Joe. You and I are all that matter. We are the important ones and I need your help.'

'You don't think you need to pay for what you've done to them?'

'My going to prison won't change anything. They're dead. Gone.' She must have seen on my face that this was the wrong answer.

'Why didn't you just disappear when you realised the police were getting close?' I asked her. 'You must have enough dough stashed away to start over somewhere else.'

'I would have, believe me, but they must've guessed I would and froze my bank accounts. You have to tell them, Joe. I'll give them everything, all the evidence they need if they just let me have my money.'

Everything fell into place. She hadn't managed to hide the cash in time, or enough of it anyway, if she wanted to disappear. That's why she had agreed to meet me. Not to relive old times, not because she loved me, but because I could be useful. Good old Joe. Nothing had changed.

'I need you to do this for me Joe.' She was close to begging now. She grabbed my lapel, pulled me close. 'We could disappear if you got me my money, or go into the witness protection programme together, get married, wasn't that what you always wanted?'

If thinking she was dead hadn't managed to kill my love for her, hearing her bargain with me, offer me herself in return for forgetting about those dead children and the innocent people she had consigned to die, did. How could I have ever loved someone so selfish and self-centred? How had I ever imagined her to be anything better?

'It's not like you've got anything you need worry about leaving behind, Joe.'

This final blow finished the conversation for me, not because she was wrong, but because she was so right. Without Cassie, the Cassie I had held a torch for, the Cassie of my imagination, of my youth, I had nothing. And that Cassie had never really existed. She backed away, seeing the hatred in my eyes.

'I'd best get going then,' She said. 'Think about it, send me a message if you change your mind.'

She turned to leave, knowing I never would. I reached out and touched her arm.

'Take care.' I said, and then she was leaving, disappearing into the fog. My last glimpse of her was of her raincoat, slowly being swallowed by the fog, and I swear I heard her hum a few bars of the song.

As I turned to head down the stairs, I realised that I could smell cigarette smoke and wondered where it was coming from. The trouble was that the fog smothered everything, vision, sound and sense of direction, it was impossible to tell where anything was, I was completely disorientated, but I knew someone was close, and it wasn't Cassie. I heard the sound of running, the Asian man I had seen before Cassie arrived pushed past me at a run, knocking me to the ground.

'Stay down!' He advised as he ran, but I quickly got to my feet and chased down the stairs after him.

I thought I was chasing the Asian man, who was chasing Cassie, but much as I believed I had taken off in the same direction, I knew I might have been heading entirely the wrong way. After what seemed like a few minutes, but was probably only one or two,

I realised I had absolutely no idea where anyone was, least of all me. I stopped and listened. I thought I could hear a scuffle, to my left, I was sure, and then a shout.

'Police! Freeze!'

I turned and ran toward the noise, trying not to slip on the greasy walkways, pounding along the path towards one of the piers. As I reached the turnstile, I heard more shouts and then two shots. Most distressing of all, I heard someone scream, a woman, I thought, and then a splash as something went in the water and I knew, I just knew, Cassie had been hurt. If you'd asked me before, I would have told you that I was not one to run towards gunfire, but in the heat of the moment, that was exactly what I did. After all, I knew I had been instrumental in setting this up, if it went wrong, I would never forgive myself.

As I ran towards where I thought the shots had been, I saw a figure running towards me. It was one of the men from Cassie's apartment, the smaller one, and he had a gun in his hand. I didn't try and stop him, I didn't care about him, I wanted to get to wherever Cassie was, but I guess he thought I would try and head him off so he hit me as he went past. I felt no real pain, and thought nothing of it, but then I stumbled and went down. That was when I saw the blood on my shirt and I realised that he had shot me. I was aware of someone chasing after him, I think it was the Asian man, and there were more shots. It took a few minutes before I was able to scramble to my feet. I put my hand over the hole in my side and pressed, hoping to stop too much blood loss. I was no longer running, it was nothing to do with being shot, it was the fear of what I was going to find that made it hard to even walk. I made my way towards the noises I could hear in front of me, someone was being pulled out of the water and then the fog lifted, as it can sometimes do, and the scene opened up in front of me.

Cassie was lying on the ground, an ominous blood stain on the front of her wet raincoat. Smaller than mine, but more deadly. The water had washed most of the blood away, I guess. Her wet hair, her beautiful hair, was fanned out around her head, water spreading out from her in lines and pink pools. Carpenter and another man were kneeling beside her. I pushed them aside and took her hand.

'Cassie?' I said. Her amber eyes were open and staring into nothing and I knew she couldn't hear me anymore.

I spent most of the night Cassie died in the emergency room, getting patched up. The shot had missed anything vital and I was going to live, whether I wanted to or not. In fact, I was treated with a certain amount of disdain, as if I shouldn't be bothering them with something so minor. I was taken from there to the precinct where they sat me in a shabby, grey interview room. I spent most of the next day going over and over what had happened with a succession of suits, and fuelled by sodas, watery coffee and candy bars. It was like a bad Hollywood movie, only there wasn't a two-way mirror, or even a camera that I could see. Perhaps I didn't even rate a recorded interview, and I certainly didn't bother with a lawyer. I no longer cared what happened to me. At one point, early on, Carpenter came in, armed with another cup of tepid caffeine.

'I'm sorry for your loss,' he said, and although I

am pretty sure he wasn't sorry that Cassie had died, his look of pity for me was sincere.

'I'm beginning to feel like one of the bad guys.' I said.

'I know.'

'I mean, I told you where we were meeting. Left you a note.'

'I know, and we appreciate that, Joe. We really do.' He didn't add that it was only good luck that he had found it in time to let his colleagues know and get the back up there in time.

'And now I feel like that got her killed.'

'She wasn't shot by us, Joe; she was killed by the cartel.

'How did they know where to find us?' I asked. 'I wasn't tailed, I made sure. There was only that Asian guy there, and he was one of yours, wasn't he?'

Carpenter nodded.

'Didn't he see the Mexicans there? Didn't he check?'

'He did check, Joe.'

There was something that Carpenter wasn't telling me and slowly it began to dawn on me.

'You weren't just there for Cassie; you wanted the cartel there too. You told them where the meet was.'

Carpenter shifted uncomfortably in his seat and I knew I was right.

'She wasn't meant to die, Joe, we wanted them all alive, it's just with all the fog, we lost them for a moment.'

'And everyone died.'

'Not everyone. You're still here, aren't you? And one of the cartel thugs will live, the one that shot you.' He smiled, a gentle smile, I think he thought I would be pleased at that. He knew that the night hadn't given him a good result, but it wasn't a disastrous one, either. They, the police, at least, had something to show for the night's work. Unlike me.

'I know this is tough, but you have to remember, she wasn't an innocent.'

He didn't add, like my wife and child, but I understood, and he was right.

'What happens next?' I asked.

'Now we have to try and work out what you might know, even if you think you know nothing. We need to try and get something good out of all this mess.'

'Like what?'

'Like any little thing that could prove useful in finding out how it happened, how she swapped the drugs, how we can tell which are good and which are useless. The fakes are everywhere and people are still dying because the doctors don't know whether they are giving patients the good stuff or shit.' His concern for his wife was etched all over his face. 'We need to know everything, Joe.'

I felt in my pocket, pulling out the two packs of tablets. What with being shot and then being in the hospital, I was amazed they were still there and intact.

'Here.' I said and pointed to the date stamp on them both, to where the 'x' in exp was smudged on one but not the other. 'The smudge on the x means it's a fake.'

He went to snatch the boxes but I held onto the good pack.

'Make sure your wife gets these, right?' And put them in his hand.

I wasn't sure if he would do that, but as he hurried out of the door, I saw his hand sneak into his pocket and there was only one pack in his fist as he went out to tell the others the information they needed.

It was a while later when I went to her funeral, for the second time. There were even fewer mourners this time round, no Ed Davey, and I wondered for a moment if there had been more people at his own affair. Sad to think about the number of people who died, unloved, unmourned and unmissed. For this funeral, the San Francisco weather had changed at last and the sun had decided to make an appearance. I felt hot and sweaty in my raincoat. Carpenter was in shirt sleeves; perhaps he had a direct line to the weather bureau. He looked a little concerned. I hadn't seen him since that night in the interview room, and he probably wasn't sure how I was going to react. After all, while I was pretty sure no one had intended for Cassie to die, he, or a member of his team had told the Mexicans where we were meeting so that they could be arrested at the scene as well. He had indirectly caused Cassie's death, even if he hadn't pulled the trigger. He still thought of her as the love of my life, he wasn't to know that at the time of her death, she was already dead to me. Our love had died when she showed no remorse for her actions, and such a callous disregard for the innocent people she had killed.

I smiled at him, to show that I harboured no hard feelings, and I truly didn't. I had written about that night, a meandering stream of consciousness piece about the whole drug fiasco and it had been cathartic if nothing else. I wasn't sure at that point if it would ever be fit to be published, in a newspaper, or as a book, as the pharmaceutical company lawyers were very keen that it shouldn't be. I had no idea then that my account of the affair would eventually win me a

Pulitzer and ensure I had my pick of jobs for the rest of my life, not to mention that I would be able to very publicly cut Martin dead at a number of events. All that was to come sometime in the future. A future that still seemed very far away.

'How's your wife?' I asked Carpenter and he smiled.

'Very well, and the baby's doing just fine too.' At least I could go to my grave feeling good about that. 'A boy.' he added. 'Thought we might just call him Joe, when he's born, if you're okay with that?'

I smiled.

'Best not.' I said. 'Joe hasn't been too lucky a name for me.'

'Your luck will change,' he seemed sincere, but how could he know? I thought about it though and standing there in the California sunshine, I began to think that maybe, just maybe he was right, and as I walked away from the graveside, I found myself humming. After all, if you're going to San Francisco, you should be sure to wear some flowers in your hair.

THE THIRD MAN

The Film

The 1949 crime drama, based on the novella of the same name written by Graham Greene, is set in post-second World War Vienna.

The Storyline

Holly Martins, an American writer of pulp westerns arrives expecting to meet his friend Harry Lime but is told he is dead. At the funeral he meets with Major Calloway, of the Royal Military Police, who gradually tries to persuade Holly Martins to leave Vienna. It comes to light that Harry Lime was stealing penicillin from the military hospital, diluting it and selling it on the black market leading to numerous and painful deaths.

The American writer then meets 'Baron Kurtz', who tells him that before he died Harry Lime asked that they care of his actress girlfriend, Anna Schmidt. Holly Martins meets her but, soon, it becomes clear that Harry Lime is alive, having faked his death. He meets Holly Martins on the Vienna Ferris Wheel.

In a dramatic finale Holly Martins shoots Harry Lime dead and is then snubbed by Anna Schmidt.

The atmospheric film owed much to the use of black and white expressionist cinematography and to the iconic music, composed and played by Anton Karas, on the zither.

In 1999, the British Film Institute voted 'The Third Man' the greatest British film of all time.

The Production

The film was co-produced and directed by the award-winning British film maker, (Sir) Carol Reed who in 1968 directed the musical 'Oliver!'.

The Stars

Holly Martins was played by US film and stage actor, Joseph Cotten, who, in 1960, received a star in the Hollywood Walk of Fame.

Harry Lime was memorably acted by Orson Welles although, for some, he is best remembered as one of the greatest film directors. In 1941, he co-wrote, produced, directed and acted in 'Citizen Kane'.

Major Calloway's part allowed the director to include the quintessential British film actor, Trevor Howard. For many, he is best remembered for playing Dr Alec Harvey in the 1945 film, 'Brief Encounter'.

Anna Schmidt was played by (Baroness) Alida Valli, an Italian actress who made over one hundred films.

The song *San Francisco (Be Sure To Wear Some Flowers In Your Hair)*: Scott Mackenzie 1967, writer John Phillips.

ABOUT THE AUTHOR

Candy Denman spent most of her life as an NHS nurse but now concentrates on writing full time. She has written extensively for television programmes such as *The Bill*, *Doctors* and *Heartbeat.* Having enjoyed writing both crime and medical stories, she decided to combine the two in her series set in Hastings. The medical stories might come from Candy's previous work, but the serial killer elements come strictly from her imagination.

www.candydenman.co.uk
www.facebook.com/CrimeCandy/
www.twitter.com/CrimeCandy

THE NOVELLA NOSTALGIA SERIES

This publishing initiative brings together the uniqueness of the novella and various memorable movies from the history of cinema.

The word 'novella' comes from the Italian for 'novel.' It has been interpreted in various ways including 'a long short story' or a 'short novel'. It can be traced back to the early renaissance in Italy and France. Giovanni Boccaccio wrote 'The Decameron' in 1353. This comprises 100 tales of ten people fleeing the Black Death. It was not until the 18th and 19th centuries that the novella emerged as a literary genre.

In 1941, the Austrian novelist Stefan Zweig wrote 'The Chess Novella' which was later renamed 'The Royal Game'. This was the inspiration for the 1960 film 'Brainwashed'.

Most modern novellas are published by Penguin Modern Classics. The various novella prizes seem to stipulate a word count of between 7,500 and 40,000. A key feature of the novella is its limited punctuation. There are no chapter headings and no breaks apart from spaces where the author needs to show a scene change.

Full details of the Novella Nostalgia series can be found at www.cityfiction.co.uk.